The
POTATO
PEOPLE

Viking
Penguin Books Australia Ltd
250 Camberwell Road,
Camberwell, Victoria 3124, Australia
Penguin Books Ltd
Harmondsworth, Middlesex, England
Penguin Putnam Inc.
375 Hudson Street, New York, New York 10014, USA
Penguin Books Canada Limited
10 Alcorn Avenue, Toronto, Ontario, Canada, M4V 3B2
Penguin Books (N.Z.) Ltd
Cnr Rosedale and Airborne Roads, Albany, Auckland, New Zealand
Penguin Books (South Africa) (Pty) Ltd
24 Sturdee Avenue, Rosebank, Johannesburg, 2196, South Africa
Penguin Books India (P) Ltd
11, Community Centre, Panchsheel Park, New Delhi, 110 017, India

First published by Penguin Books Australia, 2002

1 3 5 7 9 10 8 6 4 2

Designed by Deborah Brash/Brash Design Pty Ltd
Typeset in 22/26 pt Minion
Printed and bound by Imago Productions, Singapore

National Library of Australia
Cataloguing-in-Publication data:

Allen, Pamela.
The potato people.

ISBN 0 670 89660 8.

I. Title.

A823.3

www.puffin.com.au

The
POTATO
PEOPLE

Pamela Allen

VIKING

Every Friday, Jack's mother works.
Every Friday, Jack spends the day
with Grandma.

This is Grandma's house.

They play hide and seek.

They romp roly-poly on the ground.

They read stories.

And they eat cake.

One Friday, the clouds were big and black
and the rain dribbled down the window panes
and rattled on the tin roof.

'It's raining,' sighed Jack.

'I know,' said Grandma.

And she went to the cupboard
and brought out a big box.

Inside the box were four potatoes.

'I'm going to make a little potato man,'
said Jack.
'I'm going to make a little potato woman,'
said Grandma.

And they did.

wool

potatoes

pretty
fabric

bottle top

tooth picks

potatoes

pins with
knobs

Grandma placed them carefully on the windowsill.
'There,' said Grandma.
'There,' said Jack.
'They look pleased with each other,' said Grandma.
'We're pleased with each other, too,' said Jack.

Then one day Jack and his mother
had to go away for a while.
That Friday, Jack didn't come.
He didn't come the Friday after that,
or the Friday after that.
Lots of Fridays went by and still Jack
didn't come to visit Grandma.

Gradually the little potato people
wrinkled and withered.
Gradually their smiles
drooped and twisted.

Now Grandma called them
the little *old* potato man
and the little *old* potato woman.

She looked at herself in the mirror.
'I'm just like them,' thought Grandma,
and she sat down and she sighed.

One day a stalk sprouted on the head of
the little old man.
'He's growing horns,' thought Grandma.
Then a stalk sprouted on the head of
the little old woman.
'She's growing horns too,' thought Grandma.

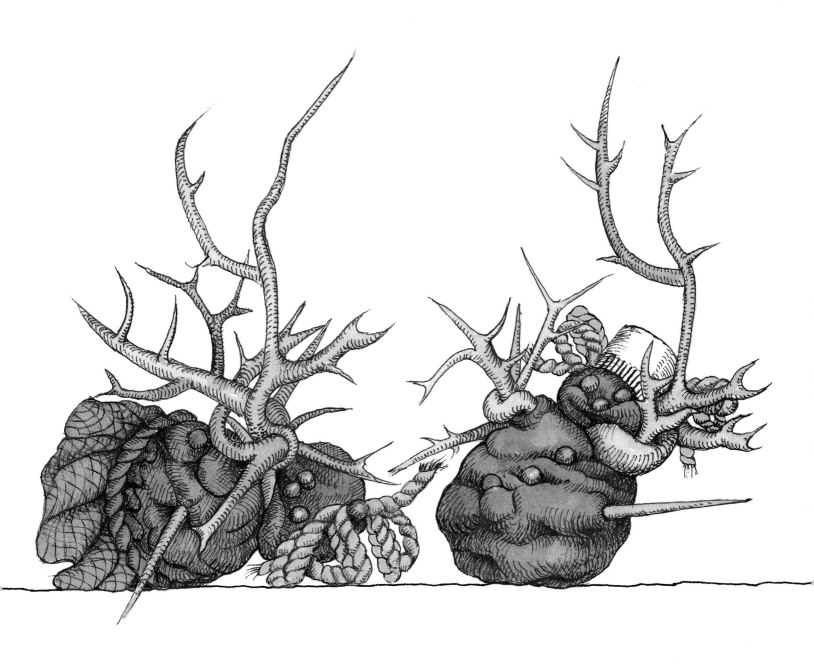

The horns grew and grew.

At last, Grandma could bear it no longer.
She said goodbye to the little old potato man
and the little old potato woman,
and she buried them outside in the compost heap.

But Jack didn't know
because Jack wasn't there.

Soon a shoot appeared above the ground.
Then another and another.
Up they grew. Up, up they grew, until . . .
they were so high that Grandma couldn't
see over the top.

'TAMBOURINES AND TREACLE TARTS!'
exclaimed Grandma.

At last, one Friday when the clouds
were big and black and the rain
dribbled down the window panes
and rattled on the tin roof,
there was a knock at the door.

'Jack!' gasped Grandma,
  and they hugged and hugged.

They played hide and seek.
They romped roly-poly on the ground.
They read stories. And they ate cake.

'Grandma?' asked Jack.
'What happened to our little potato people?'
'I buried them outside in the compost heap,'
 said Grandma, 'and they grew and grew.'
'Let's go and look,' said Jack.

So they put on their raincoats,
pulled on their gumboots,
and went out in the rain to see.

But all they could see
were the stalks,
now brown and dead,
lying on top of the ground.

So Grandma fetched a big fork
and Jack fetched a little fork
and they dug and they dug and they dug.

First Grandma found one potato,
then Jack found two potatoes.

'One potato, two potatoes, three potatoes, four.
Five potatoes, six potatoes, seven potatoes, more,'
sang Grandma.

They found big potatoes
and they found little potatoes.

Soon there were hundreds and
hundreds of potatoes.

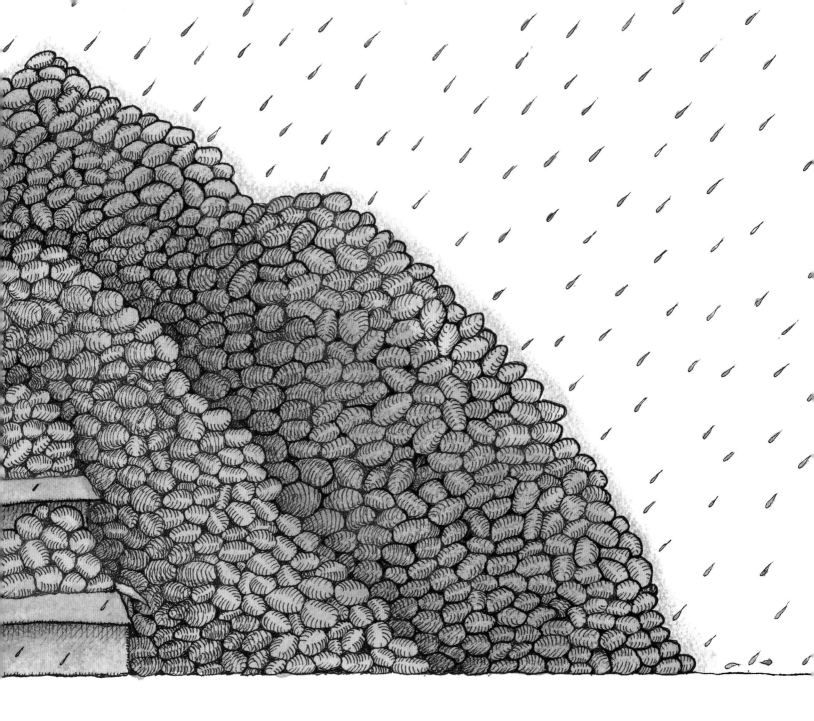

'TAMBOURINES AND TREACLE TARTS!'
exclaimed Grandma.

When there were no more potatoes left to dig,
they hung up their forks,
they took off their raincoats,

they put away their gumboots,
they washed their hands,
and Grandma dried her hair.

'Grandma?' said Jack.
'Yes?' said Grandma.
'Let's make a little potato man
and a little potato woman.'

And they did.